P9-EDZ-230

Shoshana Nambi

THE VERY BEST
SUKKAH
A STORY FROM UGANDA

ILLUSTRATED BY
Moran Yogev

Kalaniot Books
Moosic, Pennsylvania

"Shoshi! Wait for us!" calls my brother Avram. As usual, my goat, Nbilo, and I have beaten all the children to school. "I win again!" I say proudly.

My grandmother is always reminding me that life is not a competition. "Jajja," I tell her, "it's not like I always have to win the race. I just like being at the front. The view is better there!"

My brothers and I live with our grandparents in a little house surrounded by coffee trees in the Abayudaya Jewish community of Uganda.

Every Friday, I race home from school to help my jajja prepare our Shabbat meal. It's my job to mix cassava and millet flour to make the dough for the kalo bread. Then we cook the kalo, vegetables, and beans on the fire so that they are ready for us to eat when we return from synagogue.

As dusk begins to fall, the Jewish families walk to synagogue for Shabbat services.

At the synagogue I sit with my brothers. During his Shabbat talk, the rabbi reminds us that the serious Yom Kippur holiday is over. Now it is time to celebrate the Jewish people's journey through the desert to Israel: it is time for Sukkot. My brothers and I smile at each other. Sukkot is our favorite holiday!

When the service is over, everyone gathers on the lawn for kiddush. My brothers and I lay on the grass and watch the sky fill with stars. We try to count them all. Of course, I can count the highest.

"So what's the plan for our sukkah this year?" asks my little brother, David. I tell my brothers about the pile of Nsambya tree branches that I have been collecting for the roof of the hut we will build to celebrate the Sukkot holiday. "Good job, Shoshi," says Avram. "This year our sukkah is going to be the best in the village!"

Every year, families compete to create the most beautiful sukkah. People work hard to build and decorate their sukkahs, hanging local fruit like bananas, passion fruits, mangoes, pineapples, and jackfruits. By the end of the seven-day Sukkot celebration, the whole village smells like sweet, ripening fruit. All week long, people take turns visiting one another and eating in their neighbors' sukkahs.

Each sukkah looks different and each one reflects its builder's special skills and talents. Dina is the school's art teacher. Her family's sukkah is decorated with her students' colorful artwork.

Nalongo, the mother of twins, and the village seamstress, has sewn beautiful curtains and pillows for her family's sukkah.

And Moshe has a sukkah filled with bowls of brightly-colored fruits and vegetables from his own bountiful garden. He even has a dish of roasted groundnuts for people to sample as they walk by. Yum!

All year long, Daudi and his daughter, Rebecca, sell delicious samosas at a stand in the village. Daudi has saved his money to buy fancy battery-operated lights and elegant crochet trim in the big town of Mbale to decorate his sukkah.

"That's not fair," complains Sarah. "I spent weeks crocheting and Daudi just went into the store and bought everything."

"How can I compete with those sparkling lights?" sighs Yonatan.

"Daudi will definitely win the contest this year!" Isaac exclaims.

It makes me sad to hear everyone so upset.

Avram, David, and I put the finishing touches on our sukkah. We all agree that while we might not have Daudi's fancy decorations, this is the best sukkah we've ever built.

Tomorrow is the first day of Sukkot. The rabbi will make his "big walk" and choose the most beautiful sukkah. I hope he chooses ours!

But before the "big walk," the rabbi gives us his "big talk" under the mango tree. The rabbi tells us that we can compete and still feel kindness toward each other. He reminds us that the value of the sukkah competition in our community is to bring people together to admire and appreciate the beauty, creativity, and talents of our friends and families.

During Sukkot we remember the Jewish people's journey through the desert to Israel. Like those ancient Jews, we must also work together as a community.

In my heart I agree with the rabbi, but I still want our sukkah to be chosen. "Do you think we will win, Jajja?" I ask as she tucks me into bed that night. "Shoshi, you and your brothers made the best sukkah you've ever built. I think you've already won." Jajja's right, as usual, and I give her hand a little squeeze.

"Crack, boom!" I wake in the darkness to the sound of thunder and the roar of the rain pounding on the metal roof. I hear my poor little Nbilo crying and I race outside to comfort her. The wind and rain beat against the goat's pen as we snuggle up to each other and finally doze off.

In the morning the sun is shining but the storm was very destructive and many of the villagers' sukkahs are damaged. Avram, David, and I are able to make the repairs to our own sukkah easily, but not everyone is so lucky. Daudi's sukkah is totally destroyed. The battery-operated lights are smashed and the elegant crochet decorations are tangled beyond repair.

People in the village begin to talk. They feel bad because yesterday they spoke harshly about Daudi's decorations. And now his sukkah is ruined.

My brothers and I feel bad for Daudi and Rebecca as well. "We could probably spare some Nsambya tree branches," suggests Avram.

When we bring our branches to Daudi and Rebecca's house, we find a big crowd of villagers. Everybody has something to share. Dina has some of her students' artwork, Nalongo brings some pillows, and Moshe brings a dish of roasted groundnuts.

The entire village works together to help fix Daudi and Rebecca's sukkah. Daudi passes out his delicious samosas as a snack and everyone starts singing "Hinei Ma Tov— See How Good It Is." Of course, I sing the loudest.

Finally Daudi and Rebecca's sukkah is repaired and we all admire our handiwork. There are bits and pieces of every villager built into the repaired sukkah. It is a little mismatched, but everyone thinks this makes it even more beautiful.

And the rabbi agrees. Daudi and Rebecca's sukkah has won! The rabbi holds up the lulav and etrog, the important Sukkot holiday symbols. He shows us how the lulav is made with three different types of branches bound together. The many different people in our community are bound together in the same way.

"Are you sad that your sukkah didn't win the contest, Shoshi?" asks Jajja as she tucks me into bed that night.

"But I did win. We all won," I say sleepily. "EVERYONE helped rebuild Daudi and Rebecca's sukkah so EVERYONE won the contest." And as I start to doze off, I feel Jajja give my hand a little squeeze.

WHO ARE THE ABAYUDAYA?

In eastern Uganda, near the town of Mbale and a six-hour drive from the capital, Kampala, there is a community of about 2,000 people in several villages who have practiced Judaism for generations. They are known as the Abayudaya, or "People of Judah" in Luganda. Like observant Jews in the rest of the world, these Jews go to synagogue, read the Torah in Hebrew, keep kosher, and celebrate Shabbat and religious holidays.

When author Shoshana Nambi was young, Jews in Uganda lived off the land, growing cassava, millet, and beans. They would milk their cows and and let their goats loose to graze daily. Most lived without electricity and running water in thatched huts with mud walls.

In school, all instruction is done in English, although many other local languages are spoken in homes. The Abayudaya live in relative peace with their Muslim and Christian neighbors.

During the last twenty years, there have been many changes in the Abayudaya community. In Nabugoye, the center of the Jewish community, there is now an ordained rabbi, a Jewish primary school, and a high school. Some congregants now have electricity, and water is available nearby. Most people have cell phones. More young people are seeking higher education, but jobs are scarce.

The origin of the community dates back to the 1920s when the charismatic tribal leader, Semei Kakungulu, was given a Bible by British Christian missionaries. While Kakungulu was moved by the stories in both portions of the Bible, it was the Old Testament that spoke to him. He began to study and observe the Jewish laws. A few hundred tribal members followed him and the Abayudaya community was formed.

This tightly-knit group of people practiced their religion for many years in isolation. Their rituals developed organically without input from the larger Jewish world. Using only the Bible as a guide, they created a unique liturgy and set of traditions which combined their African culture with their Jewish spirituality.

For 100 years, the Abayudaya have withstood incredible hardships, but they remain steadfast in their religious practice. In the 1970s, the Ugandan dictator Idi Amin outlawed Judaism and destroyed their synagogues. But these Jews prayed in secret and the community continued. In the 1980s, the AIDS epidemic ravaged the world and was especially devastating in Sub-Saharan Africa. However, these Jews rallied, caring for the sick, and opening their homes to those who had been orphaned. And even today, while some rabbis in Israel withhold acceptance of their legitimacy, these Jews remain dedicated in their observance.

Through all of these difficulties, this unique community has remained true to their beliefs and worked to create an inclusive and egalitarian environment. We can assume, with the strength of their faith, the Abayudaya will be doing the same for the next 100 years.

GLOSSARY

ABAYUDAYA (LUGANDA): People of Judah; Jewish.

CASSAVA: A root vegetable that must be cooked; it provides Vitamin C and carbohydrates and is a staple in the Ugandan diet.

CROCHET: A type of textile created with yarn.

GROUNDNUTS: A popular snack in Africa, also known as peanuts.

KALO: Flat bread made of millet and cassava flour and cooked over a fire.

KEROSENE: A fuel oil that is burned for light or heat.

KIDDUSH (HEBREW): A blessing recited over wine or grape juice, additionally, a small meal held after religious services.

JAJJA (LUGANDA): Grandmother

LUGANDA: A language spoken in Uganda.

LULAV AND ETROG (HEBREW): The lulav is a palm branch, which is joined with myrtle and willow branches, and an etrog is a citron fruit. These four species are held and waved during Sukkot.

MILLET: A fast-growing cereal plant. Millet is ground to make flour.

NSAMBYA: A tree native to Africa. The wood of the Nsambya is particularly durable and is often used for poles and construction.

SAMOSA: A fried or baked pastry filled with beans, vegetables, or meat.

SHABBAT (HEBREW): The day of rest for the Jewish people. On Shabbat, observant Jews do not work, drive, or cook.

SUKKAH (HEBREW): Booth or hut; a temporary structure built for the celebration of Sukkot, like the temporary buildings built by the Jewish people as they traveled in the desert from Egypt to Israel.

SUKKOT (HEBREW): A Jewish holiday that celebrates the gathering of the harvest and commemorates the Jewish people's journey through the desert from Egypt to Israel.

YOM KIPPUR (HEBREW): A somber Jewish holiday when Jews reflect on their actions; a day of atonement.

MUSIC IN THE ABAYUDAYA CULTURE

In the story, the community sings the popular Hebrew hymn "Hinei Ma Tov" while they fix Daudi's sukkah. Music is an important part of Abayudaya culture and religious practice. Hymns are often set to traditional African melodies and rhythms and sung in Hebrew and Luganda. Here are the lyrics to "Hinei Ma Tov."

LUGANDA	HEBREW	HEBREW TRANSLITERATION	ENGLISH
Laba, laba	הִנֵּה מַה טוֹב וּמַה נָּעִים	Hinneh mah tov umah na'im	See how good and pleasant
Laba bwekuliokulungi	שֶׁבֶת אָחִים גַּם יַחַד	Shevet achim gam yachad	it is for brothers and sisters
bwekusanyusa			to sit down together
abaluganda okutula			

To my jajjas, for giving me a home.
To my daughter, Emunah Nasinza.
—S.N.

To my kids, Meny, Adam, and Omer.
—M.Y.

Text copyright © 2022 by Shoshana Nambi
Illustrations by Moran Yogev copyright © 2022 by Endless Mountains Publishing
Published by Kalaniot Books, an imprint of Endless Mountains Publishing Company
72 Glenmaura National Boulevard, Suite 104B, Moosic, Pennsylvania 18507
www.KalaniotBooks.com
Library of Congress Control Number: 2022931405
ISBN: 978-1-7350875-8-0
Printed in the United Sates of America
First Printing